# The Changing Earth

by Becky Olien

Consultant:
Francesca Pozzi, Research Associate
Center for International Earth Science Information Network
Columbia University

**Bridgestone Books**
an imprint of Capstone Press
Mankato, Minnesota

Bridgestone Books are published by Capstone Press
151 Good Counsel Drive, P.O. Box 669, Mankato, Minnesota 56002
http://www.capstone-press.com

Copyright © 2002 Capstone Press. All rights reserved.
No part of this book may be reproduced without written permission from the publisher.
The publisher takes no responsibility for the use of any of the materials
or methods described in this book, nor for the products thereof.
Printed in the United States of America.

*Library of Congress Cataloging-in-Publication Data*
Olien, Rebecca.
　The changing earth/by Becky Olien.
　　p. cm.—(The Bridgestone science library)
　　Includes bibliographical references and index.
　　ISBN 0-7368-0949-X
　　1. Earthquakes—Juvenile literature. 2. Volcanism—Juvenile literature. [1. Geology.
2. Earthquakes. 3. Volcanoes.] I. Title. II. Series.
QE521.3 .O4 2002
551—dc21　　　　　　　　　　　　　　　　　　　　　　　　　　　　　　　00-012591

　Summary: Discusses forces that change Earth's surface, including the movement of plates,
　　volcanoes, and earthquakes, and the effects of those forces.

**Editorial Credits**
Rebecca Glaser, editor; Karen Risch, product planning editor; Linda Clavel, designer and
　illustrator; Jeff Anderson and Deirdre Barton, photo researchers

**Photo Credits**
Archive Photos, 14
Digital Vision Ltd., 16
Digital Wisdom, globe image
Michael T. Sedam/CORBIS, 20
NASA, 4
Photri-Microstock/Atkeson, 18
Pictor/Kevin Schafer, 12
Wayne Levin/FPG International LLC, cover, 1

**Cover photo:** Lava flow, Halemaumau Volcano, Hawaii Volcanoes National Park, Hawaii

1 2 3 4 5 6 07 06 05 04 03 02

# Table of Contents

Planet Earth . . . . . . . . . . . . . . . . . . . . . . . . . . . . . 5
Earth's Layers . . . . . . . . . . . . . . . . . . . . . . . . . . . 7
Earth's Changing Surface . . . . . . . . . . . . . . . . . . . . 9
How Mountains Form. . . . . . . . . . . . . . . . . . . . . . 10
When Earth Quakes . . . . . . . . . . . . . . . . . . . . . . 13
The San Francisco Earthquake . . . . . . . . . . . . . . . 15
When Earth Erupts . . . . . . . . . . . . . . . . . . . . . . 17
Mount Saint Helens. . . . . . . . . . . . . . . . . . . . . . 19
Under the Ocean . . . . . . . . . . . . . . . . . . . . . . . 21
Hands On: Magma on the Move . . . . . . . . . . . . . 22
Words to Know . . . . . . . . . . . . . . . . . . . . . . . . 23
Read More . . . . . . . . . . . . . . . . . . . . . . . . . . . 23
Useful Addresses. . . . . . . . . . . . . . . . . . . . . . . 24
Internet Sites . . . . . . . . . . . . . . . . . . . . . . . . . 24
Index. . . . . . . . . . . . . . . . . . . . . . . . . . . . . . . 24

## Planet Earth

Earth is one of nine planets in the solar system. It is the third planet from the Sun. Earth travels around the Sun about every 365 days. It travels at a speed of about 67,000 miles (108,000 kilometers) per hour.

Scientists think the Sun and planets formed about 4.6 billion years ago. They believe gravity pulled together swirling gases and dust. Some of the dust grew so hot that it became a burning star. This star is the Sun. Other rocks and dust pulled together to form the nine planets of the solar system.

Scientists think that earthquakes shook the ground as Earth formed. Heavy metals sank to the center of Earth. Gases bubbled up from volcanoes to make air. Steam formed clouds that made rain. The rain slowly cooled the planet. As Earth cooled, the outside of the planet became hard. Rain kept falling and formed Earth's oceans.

**This photo shows Earth as seen from space.**

## Fun Fact

The deepest hole ever drilled into Earth's crust was 8 miles (13 kilometers) deep.

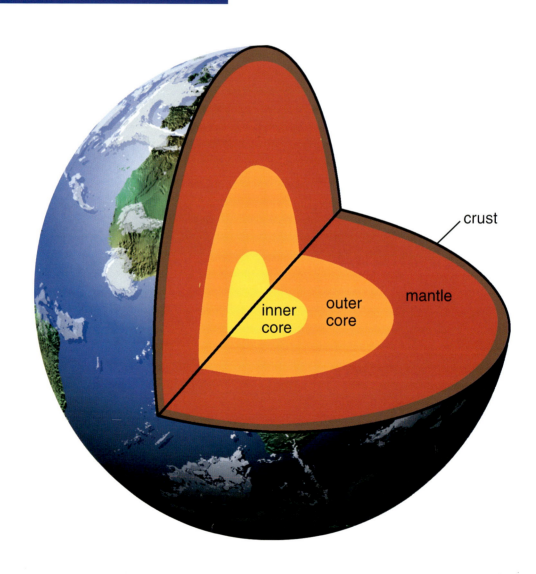

## Earth's Layers

Earth has three layers called the core, mantle, and crust. These layers become hotter closer to Earth's center.

The core is Earth's center. It is about 4,000 miles (6,400 kilometers) below the surface. Earth's core has two parts. The inner core is very hot solid iron. A liquid outer core made of iron and nickel flows around the inner core.

The mantle is above the outer core. The mantle is Earth's thickest layer. The mantle is about 1,800 miles (2,900 kilometers) thick. Most of the mantle is rock. The outer part of the mantle is a thick liquid called magma.

The outside layer of Earth is the crust. Rocks and soil make up its surface. The crust ranges from 5 to 30 miles (8 to 50 kilometers) thick. Under the ocean, the crust is only about 5 miles (8 kilometers) thick. It is 12 to 30 miles (20 to 50 kilometers) thick under land.

**Earth's layers become hotter closer to the center of Earth.**

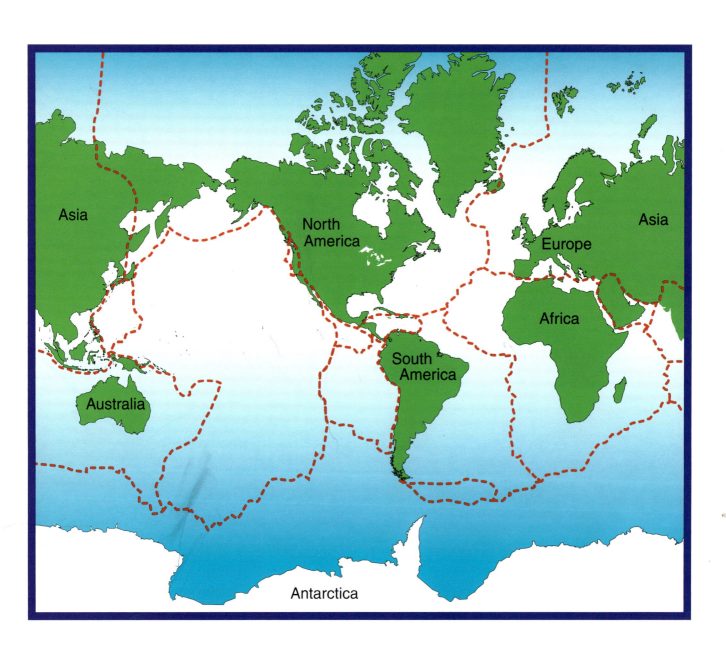

## Earth's Changing Surface

Earth's crust is not one solid piece. Eight major plates and several minor plates make up Earth's crust. These large masses of land roughly fit together to form the crust.

The plates of Earth's crust float on the thick, liquid mantle. Temperature changes in the core cause the mantle to flow quickly or slowly. Plates then move along the mantle at different speeds. They can move from 1 to 6 inches (2.5 to 15 centimeters) each year. Plates sometimes hit each other. Mountains and volcanoes form where these plates meet. Earthquakes occur when two plates rub against each other.

Geologists study how Earth's surface changes over time. They look at rocks, fossils, and the shapes of continents to learn how plates move. Some geologists believe the land once was one large continent. They think this continent broke into seven pieces as the plates moved.

**The dotted lines on this map show the edges of the plates in Earth's crust.**

# How Mountains Form

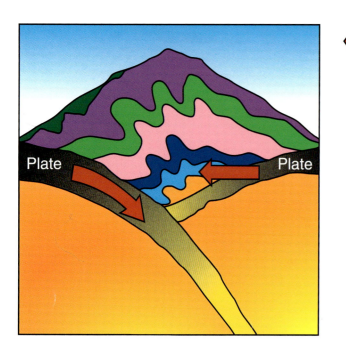

The movement of plates forms mountains and valleys in different ways. Fold mountains form when two plates push against each other. After thousands of years, the plates push rock high enough to make fold mountains.

Magma in the mantle sometimes pushes up the ground above it and forms a dome mountain.

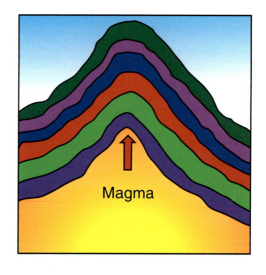

Faults in Earth's crust form mountains and valleys. Faults are large cracks in the crust where two plates meet. Land can break along a fault. One plate is pushed up to form a fault-block mountain. The other plate is pushed down to form a valley. Land sometimes breaks along two or more faults and sinks to form a rift valley.

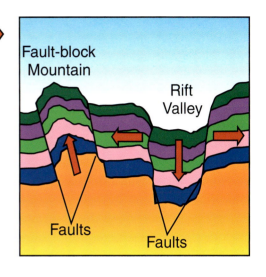

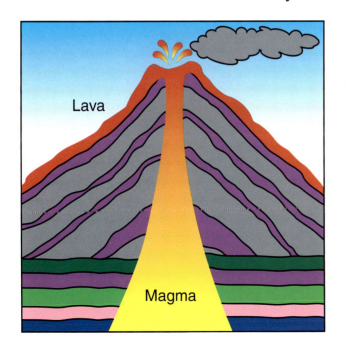

Volcanic mountains are hardened lava. This melted rock flows out of volcanoes. Lava cools and hardens when it comes into contact with air.

## What Is a Geologist?

Geologists are scientists who study Earth. They study rocks to learn how our planet formed. They record waves made by earthquakes to learn about Earth's layers. Geologists are interested in how Earth has changed. They study volcanoes and earthquakes to try to understand their causes. Geologists use what they learn to predict changes in Earth.

## When Earth Quakes

Earthquakes happen when plates move against each other. The surface near the edges of the plates then quakes. The ground shakes and rumbles during an earthquake. Some earthquakes are too small to feel. Other earthquakes are strong enough to crack roads and collapse buildings.

After an earthquake, the plates settle into their new positions. This movement may cause aftershocks. These small shocks can shake the ground many times over several days. Aftershocks sometimes cause buildings to sway.

A seismograph is an instrument that detects earthquakes and measures their power. The Richter scale rates an earthquake's strength from 0 to 9. An earthquake that is 6 or stronger is dangerous. These strong earthquakes can create landslides and break underground gas lines and water lines.

**Many earthquakes occur along the San Andreas Fault in California.**

## The San Francisco Earthquake

Two plates in California move in opposite directions. They creep past each other at a speed of only 1 inch (2.5 centimeters) a year. The San Andreas Fault is an 800-mile-long (1,290-kilometer-long) crack between the two plates.

San Francisco is a city near the San Andreas Fault. People who live in San Francisco feel many weak earthquakes each year. The crust sometimes slips along the fault, causing a strong earthquake.

The biggest earthquake in San Francisco happened on April 18, 1906. The plates moved 20 feet (6 meters) in 4 to 5 seconds and made a new crack 290 miles (467 kilometers) long.

The earthquake happened early in the morning. Gas spilled from broken pipes and caught on fire. Broken water pipes made it hard to put the fires out. More people died during the fires than during the earthquake.

**In 1906, a strong earthquake in San Francisco caused buildings to shake and shift.**

## Fun Fact
Geologists use robots to collect information in places that are too dangerous for people. Robots can gather information near volcanoes and under the ocean.

## When Earth Erupts

Most volcanoes occur where plates push together. One plate may be bent under another plate. Rocks from the bottom plate melt into magma in the mantle. The magma starts pressing up against the crust when there is too much magma.

Magma explodes from a hole called a vent when a volcano erupts. Magma runs down the sides of the volcano as lava. Lava burns everything in its path. Hot ash blows from vents and darkens the sky. Ash falls into rivers and makes thick, muddy water. Lava burns forests. Ash covers buildings.

Most volcanoes are near the edge of the Pacific Ocean. More than 500 volcanoes stand on joining plates in this area. These volcanoes make up the Ring of Fire.

Lava from volcanoes cools and hardens into rock. Lava makes new mountains or may cause mountains to grow bigger. Volcanic rock is hard. It lasts longer than other types of rock.

**Volcanoes erupt when too much pressure builds up under Earth's crust.**

## Mount Saint Helens

Mount Saint Helens is a volcano in Washington. It lies along the Ring of Fire. Until 1980, Mount Saint Helens had not erupted for more than 100 years.

In 1980, earthquakes shook Washington. Steam rose from vents in the top of Mount Saint Helens. On May 18, 1980, a strong earthquake shook the mountain.

The earthquake started an eruption. A blast of gas, steam, and rocks blew 15 miles (24 kilometers) into the air. Melting snow, ash, and rock slid down the mountain at 100 miles (161 kilometers) per hour.

The volcano caused great damage. Ash covered the ground for 300 miles (483 kilometers). Ash in the air made it hard for people to breathe. The lava burned forests and destroyed many homes. Many people and animals died.

Mount Saint Helens is still an active volcano. Geologists think Mount Saint Helens could erupt again someday.

**Mount Saint Helens erupted in 1980.**

## Fun Fact

Earthquakes and volcanoes under the ocean can make huge waves called tsunamis. The waves can be 100 feet (30 meters) high when they reach the shore.

## Under the Ocean

Oceans cover more than half of Earth. The tallest mountains, longest ridges, and deepest trenches are on the ocean floor.

Underwater volcanoes form mountains under the sea. Lava hardens quickly in cold ocean water. Volcanoes that rise above the ocean's surface are islands. The highest mountain under the ocean is about 30,000 feet (9,100 meters) tall. Its peak makes up Hawaii, one of the Hawaiian Islands.

Ridges form where plates pull apart. The Mid-Atlantic Ridge winds 47,000 miles (75,600 kilometers) along the ocean floor. Moving plates pull magma from the mantle. The magma makes a new ocean floor as it spreads from cracks in the ridge.

Trenches form where crust is dragged under a plate. The deepest place on Earth is the Mariana Trench in the Pacific Ocean. It is 35,840 feet (10,924 meters) deep.

**Oahu is one of the Hawaiian Islands formed by an underwater volcano.**

## Hands On: Magma on the Move

The upper layer of the mantle is a thick liquid. Magma is melted rock that flows within the mantle. You can learn how magma flows in the mantle.

### What You Need

1 cup cornstarch
1/2 cup cold water
1 sealable quart-sized plastic bag
two colors of liquid food coloring

### What You Do

1. Pour the cornstarch and water into a plastic bag.
2. Seal the bag and knead it with your fingers until the cornstarch and water are mixed. This mixture is like the mantle.
3. Place two drops of each color of food coloring in the bag. The colors represent magma.
4. Tip the bag and watch how the colors flow slowly through the mixture.
5. Knead the bag to move the magma. What happens as the magma is pushed together? What happens when it is pushed apart?

The food coloring flows through the mixture. Eventually, the mixture turns into a new color. Magma flows through the mantle. When magma cools, it hardens and becomes part of the mantle.

## Words to Know

**erupt** (e-RUHPT)—to suddenly burst; a volcano shoots steam, lava, and ash into the air when it erupts.
**fault** (FAWLT)—a large crack in Earth's crust where two plates meet
**gravity** (GRAV-uh-tee)—a force that pulls objects toward Earth
**lava** (LAH-vuh)—magma that comes to Earth's surface
**magma** (MAG-muh)—melted rock beneath Earth's crust
**seismograph** (SIZE-muh-graf)—an instrument that detects earthquakes and measures their power
**solar system** (SOH-lur SISS-tuhm)—the Sun and everything that orbits around it; our solar system includes the Sun, nine planets, and their moons.
**vent** (VENT)—a hole in a volcano; hot ash, steam, and lava blow out of vents from an erupting volcano

## Read More

**Kipp, Steven L.** *Earth.* The Galaxy. Mankato, Minn.: Bridgestone Books, 2000.
**Kosek, Jane Kelly**. *What's Inside Earth.* New York: PowerKids Press, 1999.
**Lassieur, Allison.** *Earthquakes.* Natural Disasters. Mankato, Minn.: Capstone Books, 2001.

## Useful Addresses

**Hawaii Volcanoes National Park**
Hawaii Island, HI 96718

**United States Geological Survey**
345 Middlefield Road
Menlo Park, CA 94025

## Internet Sites

**BrainPOP: Plate Tectonics**
http://www.brainpop.com/science/earth/platetectonics/index.weml

**How NASA Studies Land**
http://kids.earth.nasa.gov/land.htm

**Museum of the City of San Francisco**
http://www.sfmuseum.org/1906/06.html

**Volcano World's Kids' Door**
http://volcano.und.nodak.edu/vwdocs/kids/kids.html

## Index

core, 7
crust, 7, 9, 11, 15, 17, 21
earthquake, 5, 9, 13, 15, 19
fault, 11, 15
geologists, 9, 19
lava, 11, 17, 19, 21
mantle, 7, 9, 10, 17, 21
Mariana Trench, 21
Mid-Atlantic Ridge, 21
mountain, 9, 10, 11, 17, 19, 21
Mount Saint Helens, 19
ocean, 5, 7, 17, 21
planet, 5
plates, 9, 10, 11, 13, 15, 17, 21
Ring of Fire, 17, 19
San Andreas Fault, 15
solar system, 5
volcano, 5, 9, 11, 17, 19, 21